Wk Jan 18

First published in Belgium and Holland by Clavis Uitgeverij, Hasselt – Amsterdam, 2008
Copyright © 2008, Clavis Uitgeverij

English translation from the Dutch by Clavis Publishing Inc. New York
Copyright © 2009 for the English language edition: Clavis Publishing Inc. New York

Visit us on the web at www.clavisbooks.com

Looking for Christmas written and illustrated by Peggy van Gurp
Original title: *Op zoek naar Kerstmis*
Translated from the Dutch by Clavis Publishing

ISBN 978-1-60537-053-8

Manufactured in China
First Edition
10 9 8 7 6 5 4 3 2 1

Clavis Publishing supports the First Amendment and celebrates the right to read

Looking for Christmas

PEGGY VAN GURP

Clavis
NEW YORK

HIGH IN THE NORTH, in the land of the long, dark winters, lives a snowman. Lowy is his name. Lowy is a handsome snowman with all the frills: a warm hat and a woollen scarf, straw hair and a carrot nose, two shiny buttons on his chest and a full bag of food in his hand. Lowy has everything he wants. But he feels he is missing something. It's almost Christmas Eve and he would like to know what Christmas is. So he goes looking for it, looking for Christmas.

In good spirits he starts his journey. Over snow-covered fields and through dense woods he wanders, until he hears someone sniff. It's a little rabbit who is very hungry. "I'll help you," Lowy soothes, and he lifts the animal. "Nibble nabble," goes the rabbit, until there's a hole in the carrot. "Would you like to come with me?" Lowy asks. "I'm looking for Christmas."

Off they go, the two of them, for the little rabbit goes along.
Until they hear someone squeak. It's a little mouse who is
hiding in a teacup to escape a cat. "We'll help you," Lowy softly
says, and he pulls the animal by the tail. Flop, goes the cup.
"Eek!" squeaks the mouse. "Would you like to come with us?"
Lowy asks. "We're looking for Christmas."

Off they go, the three of them, for the little mouse goes along. Until they hear someone quack. It's a little duck whose foot is frozen onto the water. "We'll help you," Lowy offers right away, and he grabs the animal. Crack, goes the ice, and the duck's foot is free. "Would you like to come with us?" Lowy asks. "We're looking for Christmas."

Off they go, the four of them, for the little duck goes along.
Until they hear someone howl. It's a fox who is stuck in a trap.
Lowy wants to help, if the fox solemnly promises never to eat
other animals again. No rabbits, no mice and no ducks. "I really
won't," the fox vows. "Would you like to come with us?" Lowy
asks. "We're looking for Christmas."

Off they go, the five of them, for the fox goes along. Until they hear someone neigh. It's a horse with a roaring appetite. "We'll help you," Lowy suggests, and immediately he bends forwards. "Smick smack," goes the horse, until there isn't a stalk of straw left. "Would you like to come with us?" Lowy asks. "We're looking for Christmas."

Off they go, the six of them, for the horse goes along. Until they hear someone bray. It's a donkey who is shivering with cold. "We'll help you," Lowy says once again, and he puts his scarf around the animal. "Heehaw," the donkey sighs relieved. "Would you like to come with us?" Lowy asks. "We're looking for Christmas."

Off they go, the seven of them, for the donkey goes along. Until they hear someone chirp. It's a bird in distress. "We'll help you," Lowy reassures the bird. "Here, you can have my hat." Just in time, the three little birds climb into their new nest. While Lowy and the other animals move on, the mother bird sings a beautiful song.

The seven of them go on looking, until they hear someone snort. It's a mole in trouble. Once again, Lowy offers his help and puts the stick from his bag under a big rock to save the mole's family. All that remains are Lowy's black buttons. But when they hear someone cluck, Lowy also gives those away, to help the wood-pecker protect his nest against the cold.

Meanwhile, it's getting dark and the weather is getting worse. "I'll never find Christmas," Lowy sobs. "And I have given away everything I have. There's nothing left." But the horse says Lowy mustn't give up, and the others agree. Although they are very tired, they keep on searching, until they really can't continue any longer and see an old barn. They decide to spend the night there and take shelter from the dark and the cold.

When they're all asleep, there's a knock on the door. Everyone is awake and frightened. Lowy is the only one brave enough to open the door. Outside is a friendly man who says, "Hohoho, I am Santa Claus and I have come to tell you what Christmas means. Christmas is about kind things you do for other people. Helping, giving, sharing and forgiving. When you are kind to others, you know what Christmas is. You have found Christmas. Look around! That's why I have brought you something. Merry Christmas, my dear friends."

Lowy can't believe what has happened. That was Santa Claus at the door! And they have found Christmas after all! Together, they open the presents from Santa Claus. Everyone is in raptures. They dance and sing the whole night through. And this is how Lowy and his friends celebrate a wonderful Christmas Eve.